Seppuku

Issue VI

Seppuku

Seppuku/Joseph Fulkerson
ISBN: 979-8-9873315-8-3
Laughing Ronin Press
P.O. Box 234
Owensboro, Ky 42302
www.laughingroninpress.com

sep·pu·ku /ˈsepoōˌkoō, səˈpoōˌkoō/

(Japanese: 切腹, "cutting [the] belly"), sometimes referred to as harakiri is a form of Japanese ritual suicide by disembowelment.

It was favoured under Bushidō (warrior code) as an effective way to demonstrate the courage, self-control, and strong resolve of the samurai and to prove sincerity of purpose.

Contributors

in order of appearance

Drinking HOPPY in Piss Alley

Jason Gerrish

The street was just wide enough for Kristin and me to walk side by side, and you have to think hole in the wall, tiny bars and restaurants, izakaya with a couple tables outside each entrance further crowding the alley. And there's an outpouring of signage, all in Japanese, paper lanterns, the smell of fire, smoke and grilled meat, the feel of a street market, though most of the seating is inside, crammed into the narrow, two-story shacks.

Kristin and I try to drink and dine with the locals when we travel, and with that as our only agenda, we could have walked into any one of the izakaya on the alley. Kristin followed her nose. She chose Yoronotaki.

Once inside the front door, the man behind the cramped bar directed us upstairs where we were seated by the window and a waitress asked what we wanted to drink. An older Japanese couple seated near us were drinking HOPPY, and I pointed, for our waitress, at the brown bottle on the couple's table.

"HOPPY?" said the waitress.

"Hai," I said, and Kristin agreed to try it as well.

"Number One," said the older Japanese man near us. "Number One in Japan," he said. Then, his wife said something to him in Japanese and they began their own conversation.

The waitress delivered us a bottle of HOPPY each, along with pint glasses of ice and about three ounces of water. I assumed the beer was strong and the water allowed each customer to dilute the beer as they saw fit. So, while Kristin ordered plates of yakitori, gyoza, and fried lotus root, I poured the HOPPY into my glass, all the way to the top.

"No. No," said the older Japanese man, shaking his hand side to side, and he held up his glass, which was much lighter than mine. "White," he said.

The old man spoke in Japanese to the waitress and she brought out more pint glasses of water and ice to our table. He motioned with his hand for me to drink up the dark glass I had poured, while he poured me a new one, his way.

I tried the old man's pour, and though I noticed only a slight difference between his pour and mine, I agreed with him. "Very good," I said, "domo arigato gozaimasu."

When our waitress returned to check on us, Kristin ordered a salad of onion and ginger and I pointed to a picture-menu on the wall, at a plate of skewered livers, hearts, and kidneys.

"Number One," said the old man, agreeing with my choice. It seemed he was enjoying us, so I ordered all four of us another round of HOPPY.

Again, when the drinks came, the old man challenged my pour. He ordered another glass of ice and water for me, insisting I drink it his way. He prepared the drink and handed it to me, then raised his own glass.

"Kanpai!" he said.

And we three followed suite: "Kanpai."

Kristin and I were in no hurry. We finished our food, drank and smoked.

The couple finished their drinks and the old man got up to leave with his wife. As he walked by our table, he placed their bill in front of Kristin. "You pay," he said. "Arigato goazaimasu."

"Oh, no, no, no," Kristin said.

But the old man stepped away, and his wife was carrying on in Japanese, probably telling him to leave us alone. Of course, he returned smiling and took back his bill.

I glanced about our tables, at all the empty glasses and bottles, and feeling more than a little high, I looked over the label on the bottle of HOPPY. I couldn't find the alcohol content; it was all written in Japanese. Kristin looked up HOPPY on her iPhone.

"It's nonalcoholic beer," she said, "and it isn't water in the glass, it's Shochu."

That explained everything. But there was still much to learn. We paid our bill and headed to the Golden Gai, where we were to meet Troy and Joey, when he got off work.

Caleb Bouchard

Scar tissue exposed in the living

Scar tissue exposed in the living
room light. Props are pink and dewey,
yet hard with fermentation.
We've crossed several big
rivers at this point.
No amount of
old rags can
mop this
up.

Radio static wraps my brain like

Radio static wraps my brain like
produce. This morning I bought four
orphan avocados at
eighty-nine cents per. Dog
food emergencies
can lead to such
lovely and
unwashed
scenes.

Teach

Eddie Black

"That's the whole point. Say what you will about what it has become, but it didn't start that way. Defiance is in us, as Americans, down to our core. Right down there with all the dirty stuff, the things you never told anyone, and the things you hold true. We know our rights. We demand them. Nothing and no one will take them away from us. If they try, we call bullshit and grab the muskets and the powdered wigs."

My use of "B.S." got a rise from the students. Stu, the A-Team cornerback smirked, dumbly. Maron, a minister's kid, squirmed in her seat. She was highly offended, and I would probably hear about it from her father at the next parent teacher conference. William laughed loudly and very animated, the way kids with no friends did when looking for approval. Lindsay, a cheerleader in her second Senior year, flashed a sultry smile and a well-executed scrunch of the nose. The older she got, the harder it was for me to ignore her. I did my best to seem oblivious to her advances. The rest of the kids giggled and looked on with admiration.

So taboo, I know. What are the repercussions? Are they going to reprimand Mr. Garrett for cursing in his classroom? I can practically hear their internal conversations. I remember being a student. Everything seemed so black and white. Right and wrong. In hindsight, as a teacher now myself, it's ridiculous that we aren't to use harsh language around these kids, most of them nearing adulthood, some of them having had it thrust upon them far earlier and early. That's the world. It was just another facade of innocence the failing public school system demanded you adhere to.

The bell rang through the PA system, as it did fifty times a day, five days a week. My toes curled in my loafers. "Well, what are you waiting for? The bell dismisses you, not me." That line has killed for years. The students laughed again as they made their way out of the classroom in a hurry. "I'll see you back here after lunch." They were easy to impress. Disheveled hair and bad posture was all it took for them to think of me as the cool teacher. I wish that trick worked on women my age. William, of course, was the last one out. He was still choking out faux laughter, wanting me to witness the effect my comedy had on him. "You rock, Teach!" I smile at him as the door closes too slowly. He maintains eye contact until it's shut.

I pulled out the sliding drawer of my desk and popped the plastic insert from its place. I spread the gap carefully, not to spill the pens and things inside of it. In between the insert and the metal bottom of the drawer I retrieved a little opaque plastic baggie with a lattice of smiley faces on it. My toes were practically digging latrines in the base of my shoes. I dropped a few pebbles from the bag onto the table and smashed them under a dollar bill. I shaped the powder into three lines with my I.D. badge, before rolling the dollar into a funnel.

The first line entered my nostril. My toes relaxed, and my nasal passage burned slightly. The stuff was pretty stomped but it wasn't terrible. I had roughly forty-five minutes of me time. No pretentious staff. No pimply-faced kids. Just me and my powdered lunch. My throat became numb, and my tongue was bitter. I washed the film from it with some room temperature coffee. After a minute or two, I vacuumed the second line and massaged the cheek on the same side as my snorting nostril. After my fifteen years of use, I still couldn't tell if it enhanced the high or not. We all have our little rituals.

The straw was lined up with my last rail, and my peripherals blurred as I leaned into it. I snorted half the line when I heard an aggressive set of barks in the hallway. My shoulders tensed, and a weight dropped inside my colon like a sack of concrete mix. I sat there, dollar inside my nose, over the last half. I heard the bark again and I leapt from my chair. What day was it? It was Wednesday, right? Surely, I would have been informed about this. My mind locked in like the point of view camera from Evil Dead, searching my memories. I had been informed of this. I was told on Monday but I had been too busy fiending for it to take meaning. Drug dog day, and from the sound of it, Fido was already on the prowl.

I grabbed the baggie and twisted it shut. I could swallow it, but that would be a dangerous waste of my reserves. I looked frantically around the room. There was one empty desk near the back. Lionel Fenway's desk. He was your classic slacker, underachiever. Snakebite lip piercings, green hawk, CBGB shirt. He was the punk that referred to me as Lloyd-Uroy instead of Mr. Garrett, a mash-up between Lloyd, my first name, a sign of blatant disrespect, and corduroy, my pant material of choice. It was actually sort of clever. More importantly, he had been recently suspended for being on the wrong side of the last drug dog day himself.

I opened the lid of his desk and stuffed the bag in between the pages of an abused MAD Magazine. Something in the desk smelled awful and I closed the lid as soon as the deed was done. I ran to my desk and hurriedly ingested the remaining half line. No sooner than the last flake entered my nose, I saw the officer's shadow beneath the door. Shit. Could the dogs smell residue? I dumped the coffee on the desk and the rolled-up dollar. The officer came into the room and I stood up to keep the coffee from spilling on my Lloyd-uroys.

"Ope, you alright?" He asked in a slightly intimidating, yet friendly Midwestern way, as if I were a suspect sitting across from him in an interrogation room and the Bad Cop had already blown his stack. Maybe it was just the paranoia. Maybe it was the fact that I had Folgers on steroids all over my desk.

"Yeah. These daggum kids have me all wound up. Just spilled my coffee."

"Oh, you don't have to explain. My old man was a teacher. Kids these days, am I right?"

"You aren't kidding," I said as I soaked up the mess with a liberal amount of Kleenexes, of which the cost comes directly out of my pocket, "find anything good?"

"Oh, that Kitchner kid had a little ditchweed in his locker. Not much else though. Do you mind?"

"Not at all."

He walked the German Shepherd around all the desks, like a Gestapo on patrol. The whole thing never sat right with me. Just the government overplaying their hand with the morality clause. Most of the idiot teachers around here actually thought it was a good thing. How far we have fallen as a country, as a people, as a species!

They were at the last row of chairs and coming upon my scape-goat seat. I felt nervous, for myself and for Lionel. Although, It's not like I set up the preacher's kid. No. Just a kid exactly like I had been. I pushed the guilt away and watched helplessly with my sphincter puckered so tight you couldn't drive a needle into it with a sledgehammer. I was about as comfortable as if my uncle was giving me a back rub. The dog growled lowly at the desk. The officer was watching as closely as I was. Fido fucking barked.

The dog's nose bumped the side of the desk and slightly lifted the desk top. The rancid smell penetrated its sniffer and it dropped the lid, pulling away from the desk like it had been kicked. It seemed good enough for the handler, who nodded at me politely before leaving my classroom. The sudden silence was disorienting. I asked myself a million questions. How did that just happen? Did that just happen? Did Lionel just leave something in his desk, or was it placed there tactically? Am I giving him too much credit?

I opened the lid just enough to grab the baggie and before I could notice the resistance, I pulled it out as quickly as possible to avoid the smell. The remaining powder fluffed into the air. My spirit breaks as gravity takes hold and the drugs that were supposed to last me until my next paycheck dusts the carpet.

I fling the desktop open in a fit of anger and flip open the Mad Magazine. The smell wafts into the room. It's slightly more sufferable, now that I could see what was causing it. Or maybe it was a disturbing enough sight that my sense of smell was dulled so that my brain could use the power elsewhere. There was a little pink figure of skin, the tiny yellow beak agape. There was a bent paper clip stuck through the little bird's soft skull. I slowly lowered the lid back down. Of all the things, my baggie got caught on *that*.

Maybe it was a sign from God. I looked to the ceiling and raised an open hand to it. "Oh Lord, make me chaste... but not yet!" The current narcotics in my system would hold me over for a half hour, maybe, but I'm looking at days here. I search through a couple of desks until I find enough change for the payphone outside. No answer. I was going to have to go across town.

I knocked on the thick wooden door, standing in the same place as thousands of kids awaiting their sentencing had stood over the years. "Come in." Principal Foster was sitting at his desk. He was a heavy-set man who always reminded me of Humpty Dumpty, or at least since seeing it in one of the bathroom stalls. His bald head reflected the light from the ceiling and the plaques and certificates framed behind him caught it.

"How can I help you, Lloyd?" Principal Foster asked.

"I wish I knew the answer to that."

"I'm sorry?"

"I just blew chunks in the bathroom. I've been feeling rough all day, but it's finally come to a head. I didn't know if you wanted me to push through for the rest of the day or to go home."

"Well, finding a substi-"
I feigned a gag and put a fist up to my mouth. Foster recoiled in his chair.
"Sorry, Mike. I was just thinking about those tuna chunks and-" I gagged again. Under a look of disgust on his face, he told me to go home, that he might have to watch over the class until they found a substitute, but to go home. Anything to get me out of his office before I upchucked on any of the expensive fixtures.

The door to my Maroon Volvo creaked as it opened and shut. I lit a cigarette before even touching the ignition. I needed something to take as much of the edge off as possible, but seeing that I was older than eleven, it didn't do much. The sweat from my forehead began to weigh down my hair that was now a greasy mop obscuring my vision. I closed my eyes.

When I opened them I noticed a bright red stoplight that was approaching all too quickly and I slammed on my brakes. My headlights stuck out past the indicating line, and something rolled in the back floorboards. You have to calm down you goddamned fiend. You're going to cause a wreck, and bleeding out in the street while sober, is no way to go out.

I break away from the visceral grips of that vision and notice that while my thumbs were hooked around the steering wheel at ten and two, my other fingers alternated between flexed straight out and relaxed. I didn't dare look at the people that were in the van next to me. They probably thought Nosferatu was in the driver's seat. I felt ashamed of my state, though it quickly was overpowered by the aching from my molars down to my heels. I didn't even need a bump yet. No, this was just the angst of knowing I was dry.

My rims scraped the curb outside of Chin's apartment building. It was a shabby establishment. The floors were inch wide slats of pine that looked like baleen, or a dance studio that had been squatted in. The life of the ceiling lights were fading. Their death rattle was a dull buzz, which fit the place to a T.

I banged on the door much harder than I meant to. It sounded like the long arm of the law. I could practically hear the surrounding tenants flushing their dope as I stood there sweating. After a series of deadbolts unlocked, Chin's door cracked, only it wasn't him staring out at me. It was his roommate, Checker or Buzzard or something.

"Chin here?"

"Ummmm."

"C'mon on, man. I need to score some. Is he here?" His eyes were distant. He was stoned out of his gourd. He hummed as his brain was trying to form a sentence, which refreshed his name in my mind.

"Jesus Christ, Buzzy! Is fucking Chin here or not?"

"Hmm… I think he isn't here. Did you… hmm.. call?"

"Yeah. He didn't pick up. So he's not here?"

"I don't think so, man. Hmm."

"What the fuck does that mean? Look around."
Buzzy looked over his left shoulder. Then his right.

"Hmm… yeah. He isn't here."

I walked right down the hallway and out of the building, eating the urge to turn around and beat Buzzy's skull in with the cast iron skillet Chin kept on the oven top until his brains looked like a burst sack of ground beef. I tried to think of anyone else that I knew in Kansas City but I hadn't lived here long enough to have made many real contacts. Chin was it, except for… no. Hell no.

After a brief back and forth between me, my demons, and what was left of my morality, I realized that at this point I didn't have much of a choice. I would just have to do it and pay the consequences.

The familiar scream of metal against concrete penetrated my hearing canals. I scraped another curb while parking outside of the last resort's building. It made me grit my teeth or maybe I was already. Get in. Schmooze. Get out. Let's go.

The flooring of Irene's building wasn't as bad as Chin's. They had new tile, which was nice, even if there was a half-inch gap between the edge of it and the wall. No one takes pride in their work anymore. It's one of the many things plaguing this country. It wouldn't surprise me if America delved into a constant state of rioting and debauchery by the end of the decade. Bricks and horse tranquilizer flying through the air. The sound of a baseball bat slamming into someone's forehead-while their teeth jarr together and fall out like dominoes. Children screaming while someone slaps the thunder out of a cheap bass guitar through looted speakers.

I knocked on her door, not so much like an officer this time, but more like an orphan who was forced to return to his orphanage after his new family decided they made a mistake. Irene had just enough time to look through the peephole of her door before I heard a horrible giddy fit of laughter. "Okay calm down, Renie. You'll scare him off again."

she whispered behind the door. A few deep breaths later it swung open, bouncing against my shoulder and nearly knocking me on my ass.

"Ope, sorry! Lloyd, are you alright, baby boy?"

"I'm fine, uh, just forgot that your door opens the wrong way."

"I know! You promised to fix it, remember? Oh, you're always just so busy with those kids. I forgive you!"

She jumped into me and wrapped around my waist. Before I could react, her lips were pressed against mine and she was inside of me. Her tongue pushed mine to the back of my throat like Crow driving a Buffalo off of a cliff.

She bumped her crotch against my waist, each thrust knocking me off balance. She giggled inside of my mouth which tickled in the worst way. "Irene. Irene. Come on now." I said between the lapse of tongue and clicking of teeth.

"Irene!

"What, baby boy?"

"Do you have any?"

"Nopey. Fresh out."

"You don't have any at all? Wasn't that guy Rico supposed to bring you some?"

"Yeah, he was."

"What? He didn't show up?"

"He doesn't re-up until Saturday. "

"I can't wait that long. Do you know anyone else?"

"I know one other guy. I forget his name, but I have his address. I can call him and tell him you're going to pick some up if you want."

"I don't know this guy. Can't you do it for me?"

"Baby boy, you know I would, but I have to work at three."

"Fine. What's the address."

"Uh-uh. Not yet."

I groaned and she put her tongue in my mouth again. Her pigtails flapped against me and I was tempted to hurl both of us out her sixth story window, but instead I kiss her back.

***

I noticed that I was going sixty-five in a forty-five, so I slowed down. The whole thing was getting ridiculous. I fought an hour of traffic to get here, I had left one of my socks at Irene's, and my body was starting to betray me. My muscles were spasming, my shirt was soaking wet. There was a fear of what might happen if this guy was out too.

The neighborhood wasn't too bad. Some of the houses had little gardens and tidy lawns. Some had boarded windows and tall grass. It reminded me of my childhood neighborhood. There weren't any curbs to hit this time and I wasn't getting that nervous pre-gut feeling. I started thinking positively, even. If I didn't, I might have just chewed through my upper lip.

1312. This was it. Before I stepped onto the sidewalk, a large man opened the door and stared me down. His do rag was too tight for the melon sized head on his shoulders but I wasn't going to tell him. He had stick and poke tattoos that blended in with his skin and the friendly demeanor flaming cactus.

"You Irene's boy?"

"I guess." It hurt to say.

"You got a heater on you? A razor in your sock? Anything like that?"

"No." "You sure? 'Cause if you do, I'll be dumping little pieces of you in the Missouri."

"I'm not carrying anything. I just really need to score, man." I was running out of patience and was in desperate need of getting out of this Jim Croce song.

He looked me up and down before motioning me inside. There were little figurines all over the house. Superheroes, WWF wrestlers, NASCAR drivers, all sorts of dolls in what I could only assume were their original cases.

"He's in there."

I walked through an archway and into the kitchen. My eyes met his. His eyes met mine. The air left the room, as did all the juice left in me. My tongue felt like it weighed as much as a carburetor. He laughed the way a younger sibling did when he walked in on his big brother in bed with a girl while their parents were out. Nervous at first, then with all the power of a small-statured tyrant.

"Hey, Lloyd-uroy."

Yukio Mishima's Door to Exile

LindaAnn LoSchiavo

"I pray for an honorable death, a death for the sake of something. ...
I'll probably die in bed after a life spent dreaming of a very different end."
— Yukio Mishima

Cat lover and Japan's "Renaissance Man,"
Prolific, versatile, he was fed fame
Yet courted death, love sick for its embrace,
Gorging himself on silver gelatin
Tableaus preserved with Shinoyama's lens,
Depicting Yukio as a parade
Of dying men, a strange rehearsal for
Seppuku, door to exile, no more dreams
Tormenting him with right-wing politics,
Imperial ideals, once victory's
Laurels escaped— exhaling his pen name.

A remedy without consequences
Was the insouciant equality
Of ritual finales, red slashes,
His dagger an attentive butler, quick,
Accommodating, unpacking his shroud.

— —

Yukio Mishima (January 14, 1925 – November 25, 1970),
pseudonym of Hiraoka Kimitake, staged a dramatic and highly
publicized act of seppuku (ritual suicide by disembowelment) after
an unsuccessful attempt to incite a coup d'état in Japan

Kishin Shinoyama's macabre photo collaboration with Mishima was called "Death of a Man" [*Otoko No Shi* in Japanese], published by Rizzoli Books.

Final Words: From a balcony, Yukio shouted his last words — "Tenno Heika banzai!" (Long live His imperial Majesty) — went inside, said to a companion, "I don't think they even heard me," then plunged a sword inward. He was 45 years old.

This poem is from my WIP **"Past Tense: Poems and Portraits of Suicides."**

The Bishop

Jonathan S Baker

Chemically induced vulnerability

brought out old sadness at being ugly.

I nearly wept before my heroes

I couldn't have been happier about it.

Indian Paintbrushes

Clay Beene

In his fingertips he held a tattered Polaroid picture with "May 17, 2018" scribbled across the bottom. It was overexposed, washed out by the Oklahoma sun, but it was his favorite picture of her. Coincidentally it was the last picture he had of her too. Three days after it was taken she'd be somewhere between where he was and where she was headed. San Diego, Los Angeles, Hollywood? He wasn't sure, but hell, they're all the same right?

She looked happy. She held up a peace sign with her right hand and cocked her head left towards her shoulder. Her eyes were squinted closed. Her gentle smile was one of naivety, of someone who had yet to experience the agony this world can inflict. There was no sorrow or regret in her face, only joy and expectation. That's the smile he still pictures when he thinks of her, though it's a fabrication to veil the ugly truth. Her hair was wet and clung to her cheeks. She was wearing one of his Wrangler pearl snaps with only a couple of snaps on the bottoms closed. And because he was the one that took the picture, he knew she wasn't wearing anything else at all.

That was four years ago, and if he had a dollar for every hour he had sat on the porch with this picture in his left hand and a whiskey glass in his right, he'd be a rich man. But he wasn't a rich man, he got by. Cowboying has never been a way to get ahead in life but that never mattered to the many that came before him and it won't matter to the few that will come after. Cowboys, real cowboys, are a dying breed. You can go to any college town south of the Mason-Dixon and find thousands who like to pretend. They'll be wearing skin-tight bleached jeans, a striped golf polo with their alma mater's logo on the chest, a twenty-dollar straw hat they bought at Walmart, and a clean pair of Tecovas that have never seen dirt or a stirrup. These assholes love songs about lifted trucks, dirt roads, light beer, girls in cutoff jeans, and being country, all set to drum machine beats and electronic instruments. "Everybody wants to be a cowboy until it's time to do cowboy shit," his grandfather had always said. Ain't that the truth. He was authentic though. One of an ever-dwindling number of men who make their living on the back of a horse with a rope and a pair of wire pliers. He was a cowboy, just like his father and his grandfather before him. Six generations all told had lived, worked, and died right here in this country north of the Arkansas river. Most of them are buried in a family cemetery that sits atop a hill shaded by two-hundred-year-old post oaks. They all lie there quietly, facing east, waiting on Jesus to return in the clouds. Sometimes he'd ride up there to sit under those trees and talk to his grandfather. The man couldn't offer much advice but was always a good listener.

Like every other great love story, they met in a bar. He had gone up to Stillwater to visit a couple buddies and catch an Oklahoma State football game on a Saturday in November. He was 23, she was 20 and had a fake ID. She grew up on a ranch in west Texas known for its quarter horses. He bought her a drink, then a couple more. They talked about where they came from, horses, rodeo, cattle, music, books, and poetry. For the next year and a half, they saw each other as much as they could. It took him exactly one hour and seven minutes to drive from his porch to the parking lot of her apartment. Many times he'd shown up on her doorstep smelling of burnt hair and calf shit after branding and doctoring in the spring. That didn't bother her. She'd grab him by the collar and kiss him on the mouth as she pulled him across the threshold. Before school was out that next summer, they made the long drive to Paducah, population 1255, to pick up her horse. He told her that he wouldn't mind keeping the mare at his place and working her out as long as she'd come ride with him on the weekends every now and then. Deal. She rode in the middle the whole drive. When she got tired she'd lie her head on his shoulder and drift off to sleep. He'd look over at her, smile, and kiss her on the head, knowing he was kissing one of God's perfect creations.

When he met her father, he looked him in the eye as he offered the firm handshake of a rancher. That goes a long way in those parts. He was in the holy land of ranching history.

The Waggoner, the Matador, and the 6666 were all within a stone's throw of where he was standing. These were the huge Texas cattle ranches that he'd only read about or heard about in a Red Stegall poem, and home to some of the finest horse flesh in the world. Her mare was quite the looker. She was a light red roan that stood a touch over fifteen hands. She had two stocking feet in the rear and a wide blaze on her face. She was one of the nicest looking mares he'd ever seen. Hell of a roping horse too. The girl had been runner-up in the break-away at the state high school finals when she was a senior. She ran barrels too but didn't place. Not a bad thing, because good barrel horses are usually fucking crazy.

One evening before they headed back to Oklahoma, they saddled the mare and another bay gelding and went on a ride. They rode out through the mesquite and juniper and up a long ridge running west away from the house. They stopped at the end of the ridge which was a mesa that looked out across the ranch. It was some of the prettiest country he'd ever laid eyes on. The smoke from spring fires filled the western sky and turned the sun that homesick shade of orange. As they stared across the ranch, she told him she wanted to be an actress. This was the first time he'd ever heard about it. She said she thought she could make it. She was going to work really hard the next year and then head west like all those before her with the same dream. He didn't take her too seriously. She always had these big plans like this that would fall through. She hadn't run a marathon and she hadn't written a novel. He figured she'd graduate next year and get a job in marketing with her degree. She was a good student and would be a shoo-in at any company. He did agree with her though, that she was gorgeous and had a face for the silver screen. She smiled and looked at him with those eyes that were full of love and satisfaction. His saddle creaked with the shifting weight as he leaned over and kissed her. In that moment, everything was perfect, the world spread before them like an endless buffet, it was right there at their fingertips.

***

A yellow McDonald's wrapper blew by on the sidewalk in front of her feet. She stopped and watched it tumble and bounce into the road. It was 6:17 a.m. She walked slowly, stopping at every star she idolized. She read the name and wondered what the hell she was doing. She was grinding her teeth now. Her jaw felt tight. She passed a man leaning up against a record store window. He was asleep. Drool visibly ran down his unshaven cheek and pooled on his shoulder. It smelled like he'd pissed himself. The dark stain on his pants confirmed it. He had a cardboard sign propped up next to him that said "ANYTHING HELPS (Cash Or Weed Preferred)." All she wanted to do was sleep. But sleep rarely came, and when it did, the dreams reminded her of everything she wanted but would never have. Maybe just a couple more then. She washed them down with a drink of water and kept walking.

She reached behind her back with both arms and tied the apron around her hips. Pens, notebook, straws. She looked up into the mirror. She didn't recognize the person looking back. Heavy bags of regret formed underneath her eyes. Her skin was pale, the vascularity of her face almost visible. She was thin. Down thirty pounds from when she moved out here. Her clavicles stood prominent in the low-cut shirt she was wearing. She'd never noticed them before. The amphetamines made it hard to eat. She took a deep breath and slowly pulled the skin down from her eyes to her cheeks and down to her jaw. She exhaled as she released. Her fingers rubbed her mandible as it moved from side to side. Rummaging around in her purse she found the concealer that would hide the darkness under those eyes. Those eyes that only a few years before saw the good in people. Those eyes that used to see the future as glowing. Those eyes that had seen rape, and murder, and apathy, and greed, and all the types of bodily fluids spread out on the floor. Those eyes that couldn't unsee the things she had seen. There, that's better, the darkness was covered up. She smiled at the apparition adjacent. Time to be an actress.

Now it's the cordial greeting, how are you doing today, what will we be drinking this morning, where are you visiting from, are you ready to order, how would you like the eggs cooked, no I'm not from here I grew up in Texas, would you like some more coffee, how is everything tasting, would you like some more coffee, on one check or separate, would you like some to-go boxes, any coffee for the road, anything else I can get for y'all today, the cordial farewell, thirty times over before she clocked out at 10:30. The better you act, the better they pay. But somehow it was still never enough.

She was an actress at her second job too, but the acting wasn't as difficult. She was pretty, the clientele was drunk and horny, the tips almost made themselves. All it took was a touch on the arm or a playful glance when serving a drink and they were ready to sell their soul for a little more of her attention. Often she went home with one of these men at that dreadful hour of two. She had four hours to kill before she needed to be at her other acting gig, so she died in the arms and legs of strangers. The men would fade to black after squeezing out their juices and she was usually left with two or three hours to herself. She'd pull a book out of her purse, McGuane, Harrison, or the sort, and read while smoking Marlboro reds in her underwear. The men would wake up at lunch the next day to find and a dozen butts and a pile of ash on the floor next to the floral cushioned hotel desk chair.

And so, the cycle continued. Days into weeks into months into years. She hadn't had an audition in eight months. They always said she wasn't quite what they were looking for, or she didn't have the right energy, or the right look, or they were planning to go in a different direction with the casting.

Truth is, you could be the one in a million, but there are eight other ones in that town. At first she used the rejections to fuel the fire. I'm going to show them she thought. The failure made her more determined. But a human is nothing more than an animal, and repetitive failure will eventually break even the strongest of beasts. By now her hands were no longer steady. It was harder to apply the makeup. The egg yolks would jiggle as she held the plates. The liquids would throb in cocktail glasses as she served. The ash would fall from the cigarettes without tapping. They always talk about how sunny it is out on the west coast, but they fail to mention that you can't see the stars at night.

***

His phone lit up on the side table next to a half dozen cigarette butts, three empties and a half drank can of Coors Light. He picked it up and studied the name on the screen as it vibrated in his hand. He set down the picture. He hadn't heard her voice since she told him goodbye. After all this time, why was she calling? He figured that she had forgotten about him long ago. Assumptions are what got him in this spot in the first place though. He never thought she'd leave. She thought that he'd come with her. Two unspoken assumptions that spanned the breadth of a relationship and ultimately brought it to its knees. The image of her remained unchanged though, he still loved her after all this time. All of the girls that had come and gone since that day didn't mean a damn thing. They were just a way to suppress those smoldering, primal desires placed within us by this thing we call mother nature. They were nothing more than a life jacket that kept his nose above the waves. But his heart still belonged to her, and it always would.

"Hello?"

"Hello, are you there? Oh…. Oh my God, you actually answered."

"Of course I did."

"Oh yeah, um… well….. I don't… I don't…I'm sorry, I didn't think you answer. I don't know why I called. I didn't know who else I could."

This wasn't the voice he remembered. It seemed frail and delicate yet deep and shaky at the same time, worn raw by the past few years of her life. This was not the voice of the woman in his mind. This was the voice of someone twice her age.

"What's wrong?"

"I… I..I.. I don't know, I just…I'm just running out of time. I don't have much time left. I can't do this anymore."

She was sobbing between her words. He could hear the brokenness in her voice. Stained glass slammed onto the concrete sidewalk.

"What do you mean? What's going on?"

"I'm just at the end of my rope and… and.. and I'm slipping and I can't hold on. I'm falling apart."

She started talking faster and faster. "Nothing is what it seems out here. These people, they're not real people. I didn't make it. I've been up for three fucking days and I can't sleep. I can't fucking fall asleep. I just lay there and worry about everything and nothing all at the same time. What the fuck? What the fuck is wrong with me? What am I doing? I messed it up. It's all messed up."

She was crying uncontrollably at this point.

"Hey hey hey, slow down. What's a matter?"

Thirty seconds passed without a word. She took three deep breaths and gathered herself.

"Hello? Hey are you still there?" he asked.

"So there's this story in the Bible about this guy named Lazarus," She talked with an even tone that was composed and collected and it startled him because it was so different from only a minute before "and he was sick, so his sisters call for Jesus to come heal him."

"Yeah I know the story."

She didn't miss a beat. "Well by the time he arrives Lazarus is dead, and it says that 'Jesus wept' before he raised him from the dead. John 11:35. Shortest verse in the bible right there. I never had a hard time memorizing that one. Well, that line always confused me. Like, why was Jesus crying? He knew that he was going to bring the guy back. He knew that everything was going to be back to normal, it was going to be just fine. So why did he cry? I've been thinking about that a lot lately for some reason. I haven't even picked up a Bible since I've been here, but for the past few months I've been thinking about this story. I figured it out. I know why he wept."

"Whys that?"

"Jesus was crying for Lazarus. Lazarus was dead, he had finally left this shitty world and was in heaven or wherever. He beat the system. Jesus was crying because he knew how terrible the world is and he was about to force Lazarus to relive it. I could never see that before growing up. You don't see how fucked up everything is in a small town. I see it now. I've lived it."

She didn't say anything else, there was just a long empty silence on the other end of the line.

"Where did this all come from? Why now? Why did you call me?"

"Hey I've got to go, I'm sorry for calling." She sighed into the phone. "I'm sorry."

"Wait…."

He was cut off by the sound of the call ending.

He looked out off the porch and saw the sun slipping into the horizon. He saw the Indian Paintbrushes that only a week ago were vibrant and full of vigor. Now they were withering away, falling apart back to the earth. It was that time of year though.

Three days later he got a phone call, it was her mother. When he hung up the phone he walked to his closet and pulled down one of the two suits that he owned. The black one. He walked back into the kitchen and laid it over the chair. He would drop it off to get dry cleaned that afternoon.

Coffee

C. S. Matthews

There is a star of cream
in my coffee cup
at 9 am
and I know I will be late
cause my alarm is blaring

but I don't mind much

the air is heavy with rain
and the coffee freshly microwaved
from yesterday

makeup can hold off
while I dry nude in the shaded light
from a sun behind clouds

This poem is enough.

Beer Bottle Crooner

Jason Ryberg

One more beer bottle crooner singing along
    with the stereo on the back porch, long after
    the party is over and the bonfire has
died down, when the cops finally roll up with their
    own pretty, disco-boogy / good time
party lights going, but no sirens or guns drawn, thank
god, just a calm, cool tone from an
open window *"Hey,*
Glenn, watcha
rockin'-
out
to?" /
"Just
a
little
Ronnie James
Dio, officer." /
"Party's over, Glenn." / "Yep, party's
over." / "Go to bed, Glenn." / "Yep. Goin' to bed now, boss."

Testing for Zen

Marc Isaac Potter

(first published in Salamander Ink of Nigeria)

It's a little bit like

looking for the Higgs Boson.   Thus,

You ask yourself:

did the wisp of Zen

pass-through this life?

Part Two:

In the late morning,

after the dew has cleared,

before the heat of the day is

pronounced, Please detect

the footsteps

of a young country girl,

four, perhaps five years old.

How did she walk across this

concrete slab —

diagonally?

Or perhaps in

ever-increasing circles? Ever widening?

This concrete slab is
on a children's playground
of a big city
where she is visiting her
Cousin Anna Beth
for the first time.

Part Three:
Watching for Invisible Bird
On this spot,
sixty-three years ago
a woman came to mourn
the death of her husband
in surgery.

This little spot in Eastern Kentucky
then still known by some folks
as Catalpa,
although that village name
was already fading.

The woman's grief,
particularly acute:

During the first operation, the surgeon
had felt the man's surgery would be
of no real use, it would not save the patient;
therefore
he had not sewn the man up properly.

The man lived on and on.
Now the surgeon had to go back in and
fix his mistake. During this second surgery,
the man died on the operating table.
The man had been the husband
of this woman, crying under this weeping
willow tree.
Her name is Elizabeth Potter.

Can you tell me what bird, flew away
out of the branches of this
weeping willow tree
when Grandma's cries of pain
got to be too much?

The land upon which the tree stood
has decades ago
become a nuclear power plant.

Can you find the tiny

scratches

that the bird's precious feet

made on the bark

of that branch of the tree

as it took flight?

Storyteller

Charlotte Amelia Poe

he talks like silk ripping -

like it's expensive for him to do so

like he's giving you the opportunity of a lifetime

to sit and listen

glorious stories, all lies, of course

but he'll spin them for you nonetheless

and your mother always told you

that your tongue would turn to ashes

if you told a falsehood

and you wonder if it tastes bitter

when he weaves his fictions like some kind of universe

that's slightly to the left of our own

and a part of you

wants to clap a hand over his mouth

but you, god, you don't

because he's telling you about a world where things might be kinder

and you want to believe

if only for a minute, an hour, until the dreadful hangover of reality hits

it was never about the words, not really

it's not that easy

it's about the cost

each sentence weighted and heavy

dropping into your lungs as you breathe it in

pulling you down and down and down

and if this is what drowning is, then, well

you never were afraid of the water

not the way you should have been

and okay, maybe this isn't self destruction

but when he turns to you and says he can tell you

everything about yourself

oh, but don't you lean forward,

waiting for the annihilation that follows.

Wren McKinley

Empyrean state
Heavenly orbs shine brightly
Rest on atmosphere

Electric charged sky
Crimson in tonality
Obscuring the sun

Silent trees reaching
Air stagnating leaves rustling
A path to sunlight

Fragments from the Life of Angus Adams
Mark Keane

Angus Adams had no eyebrows. It meant trouble for him at school. His classmates weren't interested in the medical cause or complexities of selective alopecia. Here was a way to make his life hell, handed to them on a plate. They called him *baldy eyes*, which was shortened to *baldy*. The name stuck even though Angus had been blessed with a full head of wiry black hair.

Angus was a musical child. His parents forked out good money on lessons in piano, violin and flute. Young Angus showed a particular flair for the violin, and by the age of ten could knock out tricky Bach and Paganini pieces. When his father's rural relatives visited, he entertained them with intricate jigs and reels.

After secondary school, Angus attended a conservatoire and earned an MA in Musicology. This led to a place among the violins in The National Symphony Orchestra.

His father welcomed the news.

"That's steady employment," he said. "You had us worried about your future."

Adams senior presented Angus with a watch—Swiss made, white dial, Roman numerals, and day and date windows.

"Now," he told his son, "you'll always be on time."

His first week in the Orchestra, returning home from rehearsals Angus decided to take a shortcut through an area of rundown flats. A mistake, he realised too late, when he came across a cluster of yobbos loitering under a lamppost. Two of them blocked his path.

"Where do you think you're goin'?" asked one, sunken eyes and chin covered in pustules ready to pop.

"Why do you look so surprised?" asked the other, his bony face contemptuous. He nudged his mate and let out a nasty laugh. "What the fuck, this freak doesn't have any eyebrows."

They grabbed the violin, and gave Angus a good kicking. Then they amused themselves, plucking the strings and dancing about. Tiring of that, they smashed the violin to pieces and threw the case into a communal bin.

The following day, a bin man rescued the case and brought it to a pawnshop. He got enough money for three flagons of cider.

From that day on, Angus avoided the shortcut. He dawdled in the auditorium lobby after rehearsals, waiting for an opportunity to accompany Clarice on her way home. She played percussion—glockenspiel, snare drums and cymbals.

Inordinately shy, Clarice released her inner anxiety by pounding and banging her instruments. What remained was gentleness and kindness, which she bestowed on Angus. He, in turn, showered her with tokens of his affection, including an engagement ring.

They married in Saint Anthony's church; she declared the marriage vows, accepted the priest's blessing, and became Clarice Adams.

Clarice died in a swimming accident. Five blissful years of marriage had passed in an instant. Angus would never marry again.

On the morning of the accident, he weighed himself on the bathroom scale; the needle pointed to seventy-three kilograms. A week after the funeral, he weighed seventy kilograms. His happiness with Clarice came to three kilograms.

When Angus turned forty, he had sufficient savings and decided to do something about his missing eyebrows. The oboist in the orchestra put him in contact with a cosmetic surgeon who had developed a procedure for eyebrow transplant.

Angus grew a moustache in preparation for the process of hair replanting. The new hair took root, and Angus had a thick moustache over each eye, which the barber trimmed and shaped once a month.

After twenty-two years of reliable service, his watch stopped working. He took it to a watchmaker to be repaired. The watch gave accurate time for another year before stopping again. Angus didn't bother having it fixed but continued wearing it.

People sometimes asked, "What's the point of wearing a broken watch?"

Angus would regard the questioner with expressionless eyes, surmounted by his moustache-eyebrows.

"It was a present from my father," he'd say.

Working watch or stopped watch, Angus was never late for an appointment.

The clock in the kitchen had spoons for hands. Clarice had found it in a Bric-a-Brac shop.

"I think it's so cute," she often remarked.

Angus thought it was a hideous thing, much like the furniture—glass tables, spongy couches and wicker rocking-chairs. Clarice had poor taste when it came to fixtures and furniture and art and books. Her qualities were gentleness and percussion.

Angus couldn't bring himself to throw away items he associated with her. In time, he refused to discard any possession—dry pens, cracked mugs, old newspapers or dead batteries.

One spring morning, the buzzing of two bluebottles drew Angus to the kitchen window. One fly was larger than the other. The smaller bluebottle gripped a crumb it must have taken from Angus' plate. They flew back and forth, colliding against the window pane. The large bluebottle danced on the small one. Angus watched, absorbed and appalled by the persistence of the large bluebottle.

He went into the garden and lay on the grass, his face uplifted to accept the caress of the pale sun. His brain buzzed with the sound of the bluebottles. He imagined them, in flight and landing, the large fly atop the small one.

Angus took to examining his past and assessing his present. He attended confession at Saint Anthony's, the first time he'd been in the church since Clarice's funeral.

"It's twenty-five years since my last confession."

"What is it you wish to confess?" asked the priest.

Angus could make out a hooked nose and jowly face through the mesh that separated him from his confessor.

"I haven't done enough," he said. "I've been too passive."

"Are you prepared to confess your sins?"

"I long to be somewhere else. Somewhere I miss so much it makes me sick with yearning though I've never been there and don't even know where it is."

Angus left the confessional dissatisfied and blamed himself for not expressing his thoughts properly.

The Orchestra had completed a cycle of Hayden and Mendelssohn recitals. Angus sat with Richard, the clarinetist, in the Concert Hall bar.

"Can I ask you something?"

Richard nodded and took a sip of whiskey.

"Do you believe in God?"

Richard hesitated. "There are three questions you should never ask, as you can never be sure of an honest answer. One, how much money do you have? Two, what do you think of my violin playing? Three, do you believe in God?" Richard swirled the whiskey in his glass. "Do *you* believe in God?"

Angus pursed his lips. "It's probably better to ask if I *want* to believe in God or want to *not* believe in God."

In his late fifties, Angus became the oldest member of the Orchestra, and had seen many lead violinists come and go. One October, he took a train to join his fellow musicians for a concert of Shostakovich in a provincial town.

Something about the train conductor tugged at his memory. He examined the man's sharp features and felt offended by his brusque manner. Angus wasn't to know the conductor was the son of one of the assailants who had beaten him all those years ago and smashed his violin. Nor could he have known that the old fogey sitting across the aisle, and coughing into a handkerchief, was the bin man who had hocked his violin case for three flagons of cider.

On turning sixty-five, Angus retired from the Orchestra. At first, he missed the routine, the ritual of performance if not the company of the musicians.

In due course, any sense of loss faded, and he took up a new routine. He watched snooker on TV, tried his hand at preparing exotic meals from cookbooks, started baking, and made his own ice-cream.

He took walks along the esplanade by the sea in the summer breeze and the heartening redolence of autumn. A five-kilometre walk, then two, then one with a walking stick. Finally, a fifty-metre shuffle behind a walking frame.

The hairs of his moustache-eyebrows fell out and didn't grow back. His wiry grey hair thinned and receded. The aging *baldy* Angus Adams was forgetful. One day, he neglected to add water to a pot he put on the stove, and the enamel cracked. Another day, he forgot to turn off the tap and flooded the bathroom.

Angus moved into a nursing home. Each morning, the caregiver told him what day it was and what he had done the day before. She gave him his pills. As soon as she left, he struggled to remember her name or what she had said. But he remembered the watch that was a present from his father, and the clock with spoons for hands. And he remembered his stolen violin and the kicking he had received, and his wife Clarice, and Richard the clarinetist, and the priest in confession with the hooked nose, and the two bluebottles.

WHERE THE NIGHT TRIPPERS ARE

Kevin Ridgeway

hidden in a mausoleum

of ghostly remembrance

alongside the speeding

freeway of my mind

are the cool vibes of 3 AM

lost beyond every midnight

when sleep wasn't an option,

daydreaming

hipster cryptkeepers

laughing in the dark

at the drops of rain

falling on my head,

stormy memories

from cloudy skies

dancing to music

not a single soul has

ever played before.

WORRY LINES

Kevin Ridgeway

I discovered them

on my forehead in the mirror

consequences of brooding

over so many wrinkles in time

now everyone can see

how heavy it is to carry around

a mind like the one I've got

battle scars that begin to show

my entire story without me

having to say a word

Rider

Kathleen Denizard

Midday heat soared from narrow pavement and choked the air like rising smoke

When the rider scraped his Harley to a stop at the Dry Creek Diner

She saw him, an Adonis of rock-hard bronze and sweat

Braced against the soda machine pulling out a couple of Pepsi's

His blue bandana was knotted above blue eyes that focused solely on the menu

Not seeing her adjust the strap of her apron

Not amused by her twisting an unruly wisp of hair

Not caring where her thoughts were leading

Chicken tacos and hot sauce for the road

Could she get him anything else?

Risking a hope, she jotted her cell number on the check

Into the afternoon haze, the rider bumped up the kickstand and sank in the bike

A passenger dressed like his twin slid onto the seat behind him

"Sure, baby, I'll call you," he muttered

And let the rev of the engine stir the tab into a dust storm

Death Scene with Pickles

Preacher Allgood

crap and shit and all those words. a heart attack right here in the condiment aisle of america's favorite super-store. tomorrow was my night off. but tonight, coronary of the fatal kind while I clutch a case of gherkins to my chest. serves me right, the life I've led. straight up karma, the mistakes I've made, the people I've disappointed.

look at that teeny bopper with her short blue shorts and long slim legs. she stares at me like I'm something her rich and brave daddy would put out of its misery with a stomp to the throat. but he's not here and I fumble the pickles back on the pallet. god forbid, I should drop them and create a huge spill for the homicidal maniac we call a maintenance man to clean up. plus, I don't want to slog through those endless damaged inventory forms corporate requires. not on my way to the morgue.

here comes a manager. that's all I need on my way out. One of those brainless twits to accuse me of malingering. I've slumped to the floor. he bends over me. his breath stinks of booze, mouthwash, and bloodless corporate lingo. that stench wafts over me as I fade away. it will haunt my nostrils for eternity.

Try

Lee Eustace

Try. Just Try, I reminded myself.

The trees in the driveway rustled when the garage door opened.

"Do it quieter. Quieter! Or you'll wake 'em."

I leaned into dad's car, put it in neutral, and pushed until it rolled beyond the pillars and into the street. "Get in!" I said as I flung open the driver's door and headed for the passenger's side.

"Yes, man!" Jacob cheered as he took the wheel. "Remind me to never bet against you again!"

"It's no wonder my parents think you're a bad influence."

"They've thought that since the time I learned to copy your mom's cursive in fourth grade. Remember?

Jacob's words blurred as I thought of Progressive Field. The Cleveland Indians. Baseball. The American sports that my dad disapproved of so much. The sounds from the radio entered and exited my ears like static while I dreamed of the big game that afternoon.

The first time I'd get to be there.

It was an unfamiliar destination along familiar city roads. As we drove, I remembered our weekend walks from downtown to Ontario Street. Mom and Li would come too. We'd fill our trolleys with groceries because we had no car back then.

Not even the shitty green dodge that Jacob and I cruised in that afternoon. Just the trolleys and dad's advisory words to Li and me: "Focus on your studies. Take up more community activities. Not sports. It won't be easy to get into Ohio State. Great medical school there."

Spooked by that memory, I checked again that my phone was turned off in case they had a tracking app on it. I held the device tightly in my hand as if I could squeeze away its existence.

Just then, Jacob turned the corner sharply and the slipped from my grip. I stooped down to retrieve it but my hand caught on a crumpled yellow scrap of paper. The paper was the type you'd find in any office stationery press. It was folded and double sealed at the edges like it either wasn't supposed to be read or its contents had been long forgotten.

I unfolded it and the words shifted around my brain like alphabet soup. "Room 203. 8pm. Be ready x"

I fell more silent in my words and my thoughts than I had ever been before. Jacob's words echoed in the space between us as if they were transmitted by sonar. As if he were trying to find my location: "Are you okay, man?"

I gulped and clenched my fists. Hard. The edges of the paper left a mark on my skin.

Together

Molly Glinski

There will be a Sunday morning

Years from now, bound in moments of solace before the world wakes.

I will watch the fragments of passed lives in the cracks of the curtains, moments before I get up to make the coffee. The friends I had dreamed about the night before have gotten blurrier in the last year or so, as though we are but moving vehicles in the depth of a rush hour in a rear view mirror. My memories with them will die soon when I speak about them for the last time. I allow the nights I spent staring at stars through vomit-polluted puddles to dissipate with the winter evenings they were born in. A bitter December in my memory.

The career I wanted when I was twenty-one is being ranked as one of the highest earners in 2032 in the paper. The kitchen I wanted at twenty-four is on page fifteen of the lifestyle foldout that no one reads. I know I will have gotten jam on one of the page corners. Quietly, I will question it all, slowly, as I am putting our breakfast together- What I could have been if I had curated my life for the consumption of others.

But my musings will be interrupted the snag on my stair carpet that I almost trip over every morning as I carry our breakfast up to the bedroom. Two bagels. Two bowls of cereal. Two coffees. The same as every Sunday. Together. And I will realise that I don't aspire to anything, I don't need for anything in this world unless it is growing old with you.

Count Off and Out

Steve Brisendine

One
more song, she pleads
as the guitarist unplugs
          and it's

two
minutes until the noise
ordinance kicks in;
          they've got

three
fives and a handful of
singles in the tip jar
          and the

four
strings of her bass echo,
yield to hums of talk and
          traffic

No One Wants to Clean Up Being Blind to the Sky

Benito Vila

Tripping back through the zodiac, myth by myth, star by star, each cycle, each history telling secrets as obvious as the sun, as subtle as Mother Goose. The cosmos innately knows its maker, and sings their song clearly, freely, without wondering what part of its maker to worship or thank. Mankind likes to think far more than listen, likes to use yesterday to make sense of today and likes to carry resentments as far as it can, even though there's little benefit to the species in doing life like that. Alice thrives in Wonderland, discards her preconceptions, her biases, and becomes deathless, patient and radiant. Wile E. Coyote will not quit. Mickey Mouse is happiest when he's home, asleep, next to Minnie, cute suburbanites, so busy fixing, doing, getting so tired they forget to fuck. Bugs Bunny cross-dresses, whistles, laughs and mixes up words in his own way to make sense of what's happening. Bugs befriends his monsters and his enemies, kisses them all. It doesn't matter to him who anyone cares for or who anyone has sex with. Hey, Diddle Diddle ain't about no cat or no fiddle. Orion's belt ain't no belt. The little red hood represents more than one little girl. The fishes yield to the water bearer, the water bearer yields to the sea goat, the archer follows. Real healing begins when the path of heaven is complete. To be emotionally driven or spiritually guided is the first choice to be made. To be aware of who, what, where and when is the how of it. Lay down those burdens, unbind them and set them free. Will's Caesar, Hamlet and Othello would not wait, would not listen and left a mess. No one wants to clean up being blind to the sky.

Bio

Jason Gerrish writes poetry and short fiction. He has been published in Seppuku, Paper & Ink Literary Zine, Alien Buddha, Bold Monkey Review, and Horror Sleaze Trash, among others. Jason's first book of poetry titled Old State Road, in collaboration with photographer Brad Daulton, was published by UnCollected Press in 2021.

Caleb Bouchard is the author of The Satirist (Suburban Drunk Press 2023). His poems have recently appeared in The Laurel Review, Litro, Rejection Letters, and Salamander. He lives outside Atlanta where he teaches college-level writing. Find him on IG: @calebbouchard.

Eddie Black is a former professional wrestler and arms dealer. He has written three poetry books (Uncooked and Undignified, Hound Dog, Between Yips of Victory and Guilt) and two screenplays. Currently, he is looking for a publisher for a collection of short stories about the hard life. He is constantly traveling, usually getting caught up in the American underbelly. It's a good thing he likes it there.

LindaAnn LoSchiavo Native New Yorker LindaAnn LoSchiavo, a four-time nominee for The Pushcart Prize, has also been nominated for Best of the Net, the Rhysling Award, and Dwarf Stars. Elgin Award winner "A Route Obscure and Lonely" (Wapshott, 2019), "Women Who Were Warned" (Cerasus, 2022), IPPY Award nominee "Messengers of the Macabre" (Audience Askew, 2022), "Apprenticed to the Night" (UniVerse Press, 2023], and "Felones de Se: Poems about Suicide" (Ukiyoto, 2023) are her latest poetry titles. She is a member of SFPA, The British Fantasy Society, and The Dramatists Guild. Twitter: @Mae_Westside / LindaAnn Literary: https://www.youtube.com/channel/UCHm1NZIlTZybLTFA44wwdfg

Jonathan S Baker has most of their teeth left and is the author of some poetry. Their most recent works include Thump! Thump! (Laughing Ronin Press, 2023) and the upcoming Pressure (two key customs, 2023).

Clay Beene was born and raised in Northeast Oklahoma and currently resides there after spending a few years in the Pacific Northwest. He continues to study the art of storytelling because stories are the only things that last.
You can find Clay on IG: @OfCowboysAndCoyotes.

C.S. Matthews is the coauthor of Fearful Architecture an editor for The Grindstone Magazine, as well as the cover artist for many a book. Having cut her teeth as an independent journalist and medic during the 2020 protests, their work focuses heavily on activism, their indigeneity, trauma, and her experiences being transgender.

Jason Ryberg is the author of fifteen books of poetry, six screenplays, a few short stories, a box full of folders, notebooks and scraps of paper that could one day be (loosely) construed as a novel, and a couple of angry letters to various magazine and newspaper editors.
He is currently an artist-in-residence at both The Prospero Institute of Disquieted P/o/e/t/i/c/s and the Osage Arts Community and is an editor and designer at Spartan Books. His latest collection of poems is The Great American Pyramid Scheme (co-authored with W.E. Leathem, Tim Tarkelly and Mack Thorn, OAC Books, 2022). He lives part-time in Kansas City, MO with a rooster named Little Red and a billygoat named Giuseppe and part-time somewhere in the Ozarks, near the Gasconade River, where there are also many strange and wonderful woodland critters.

Marc Isaac Potter (we/they/them) … is a differently abled writer living in the SF Bay Area.
Marc's interests include blogging by email and Zen.
They have been published in Fiery Scribe Review,

Feral A Journal of Poetry and Art, Poetic Sun Poetry, and Provenance Journal. Twitter is @marcisaacpotter.

Charlotte Amelia Poe (they/them) is an autistic nonbinary author from England. Their first book, How To Be Autistic, was published in 2019. Their debut novel, The Language Of Dead Flowers, was published in September 2022. Their second novel, Ghost Towns, was self-published in 2023. Their second memoir, (currently untitled), will be published in 2024.

Wren McKinley is a musician, artist, and writer. They've recorded, toured, and played professionally as a musician most of their life. The past ten years, they've gotten back into writing, especially haiku.

Mark Keane has taught for many years in universities in North America and the UK. Recent short story fiction has appeared in Muleskinner Journal, Shooter, Black Moon Magazine, untethered, Liennek Journal, Granfalloon, Samjoko, upstreet, Liquid Imagination, Into the Void, Night Picnic, Firewords, Dog and Vile Short Fiction, the Dark Lane and What Monsters Do for Love anthologies, and Bards and Sages Best Indie Speculative Fiction. He lives in Edinburgh (Scotland).

Kevin Ridgeway's books include Too Young to Know (Stubborn Mule Press) Invasion of the Shadow People (Luchador Press) and A Ludicrous Split 2 (with Gabriel Ricard, Back of the Class Press). His work has appeared in The Paterson Literary Review, Slipstream, Chiron Review, Nerve Cowboy, Main Street Rag, San Pedro River Review, Cultural Daily, Plainsongs, Spillway, The Cape Rock, Trailer Park Quarterly and The American Journal of Poetry, among others. A Pushcart and Best of the Net nominee, he lives and writes in Long Beach, CA.

Kathleen Denizard There is pure joy in sharing my writing, in relating the many wonders of life as a mature observer of people and nature drawing on my background in teaching and social services. Living on the seacoast of Massachusetts has significant influence in my poetry endeavors, inspiring me to set my thoughts into words universally and sincerely. My work has been published domestically and internationally.

Preacher Allgood is the founder of The Temple of the God Awful. It's part cult, part tax dodge and one hell of an ego trip.

Lee Eustace is a writer and a poet who is often based in Dublin, Ireland and sometimes based wherever his backpack will take him. Lee's work (poetry, fiction, creative nonfiction) has reached an international audience on platforms such as Please See Me and SeaGlass Literary (United States), Eunoia Review (Singapore), and Free_The_Verse, Apricot Press and London Wildlife Trust (United Kingdom). He is also recently published in Ireland in The Martello Journal. Additionally, Lee is well known in the local community for a set of creative nonfiction works "Bread and Jam" which he penned based on the lives of the members in a local community centre for the elderly. Follow Lee's progress on IG: @creativeleestorytelling

Molly Glinski (She/Her) is a writer based in London, England. She is the founder and editor of Late Britain Zine at @latebritainzine on Instagram. Her work is mostly influenced by current affairs and human relationships. Her debut chapbook 'Another Girl' was published by Bottlecap Press in late 2022.

Steve Brisendine is a writer, poet, occasional artist, recovering journalist – lives and works in Mission, Kansas. His most recent collections are Salt Holds No Secret But This (Spartan Press, 2022) and To Dance with Cassiopeia and Die (Alien Buddha Press, 2022), a "collaboration" with his former pen name of Stephen Clay Dearborn. His work has appeared in Modern Haiku, Flint Hills Review, Connecticut River Review and other journals and anthologies.
Write to him at steve.brisendine@live.com

Benito Vila lives in a remote fishing village on Mexico's Pacific coast. He first had his poetry published in 2020 in Love Love, an underground magazine based in Paris. His other published work includes the editing Of Myth & Men, a narrative cut-up of poet Charles Plymell's email correspondence (for Bottle of Smoke Press) and creating profiles of "counterculture" instigators for pleasekillme.com and legsville.com. 2023 finds him working on a second email book for Charles Plymell and looking forward to a set of record releases for which he's written and edited liner notes—a new opera from Mike Watt and three albums from Peter Stampfel.

www.ingramcontent.com/pod-product-compliance
Lightning Source LLC
Chambersburg PA
CBHW070645130626
46555CB00006B/2716